Marvin K. Mooney Will you PLEASE GO NOW!

By Dr. Seuss

DISCARDED
from Iowa City Public Library

IOWA CITY
OCT - - 2008
PUBLIC LIBRARY

A Bright & Early Book

RANDOM HOUSE / NEW YORK

TM & © 1972 by Dr. Seuss Enterprises, L.P. All rights reserved under International and Pan-American Copyright Conventions. Published in the United States by Random House, Inc., New York, and simultaneously in Canada by Random House of Canada Limited, Toronto.

Library of Congress Cataloging-in-Publication Data:
Seuss, Dr.   Marvin K. Mooney, will you please go now!   (A Bright and early book, #13)
SUMMARY: Suggests in rhyme a number of ways for Marvin K. Mooney to travel as long as he gets going—now!
ISBN: 0-394-82490-3 (trade) ; 0-394-92490-8 (lib. bdg.)
(1. Stories in rhyme. 2. Fantasy) I. Title PZ8.3.S477Mar (E) 72-1441

Manufactured in the United States of America   78

The
time
has come.

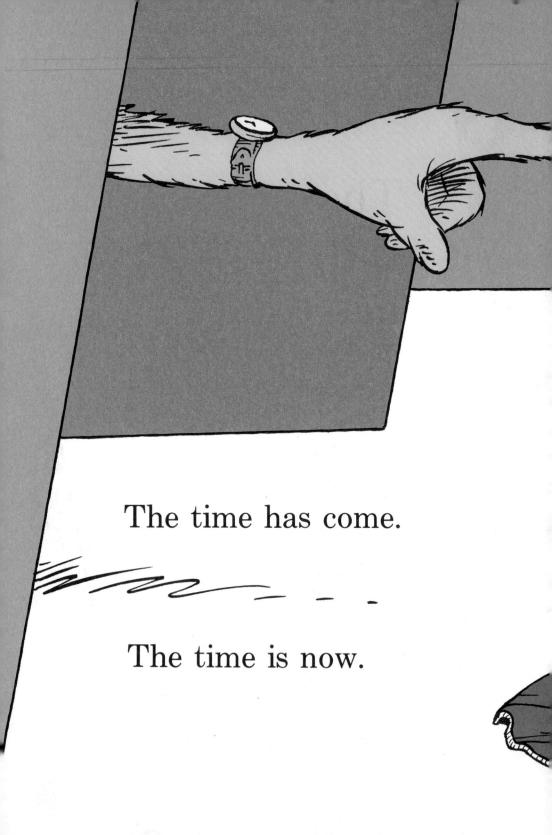

The time has come.

The time is now.

Just go.
Go.
GO!
I don't care how.

You can go by foot.

You can go
by cow.

Marvin K. Mooney,
will you
please go now!

You can go
on skates.

You can go
on skis.

You can go
in a hat.

But
please go.
Please!

I don't care.
You can go
by bike.

You can go
on a Zike-Bike
if you like.

If you like
you can go
in an old blue shoe.

Just go, go, GO!
Please do, do, DO!

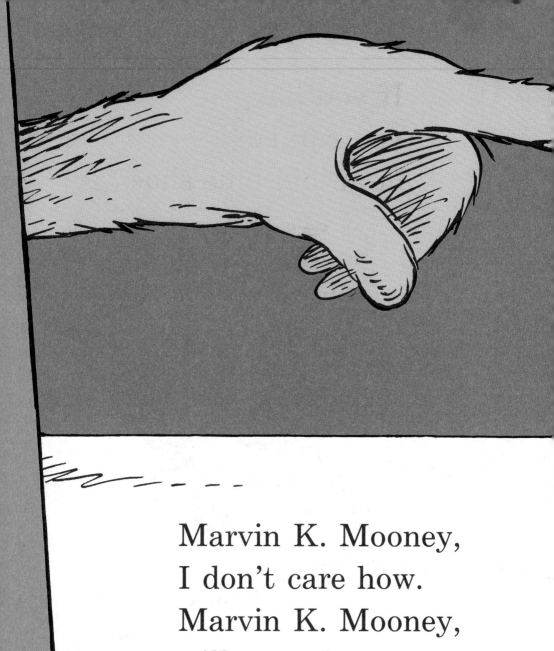

Marvin K. Mooney,
I don't care how.
Marvin K. Mooney,
will you please
GO NOW!

You can go on stilts.

You can go by fish.

You can go
in a Crunk-Car
if you wish.

If you wish
you may go
by lion's tail.

Or stamp yourself
and go by mail.

Marvin K. Mooney!
Don't you know
the time has come
to go, Go, GO!

Get on your way!
Please, Marvin K.!
You might like going
In a Zumble-Zay.

You can go
by balloon ...

... or broomstick.

OR

You can go
by camel
in a
bureau drawer.

You can go by Bumble-Boat ...

... or jet.

I don't care
how you go.

Just GET!

Get yourself a Ga-Zoom.

You can go with a . . . . .

Marvin, Marvin, Marvin!
Will you leave this room!

Marvin K. Mooney!
I don't care HOW.

Marvin K. Mooney!
Will you please
GO NOW!

I said

GO

and

GO

I meant. . . .

The time had come.
SO ...
Marvin WENT.